Nina's Treasures

Stefan Czernecki and Timothy Rhodes

Illustrated by
Stefan Czernecki

HYPERION PAPERBACKS FOR CHILDREN
NEW YORK

In memory of Maria Czernecki

Originally published by Sterling Publishing Co., Inc.,
387 Park Avenue South, New York, New York 10016 and
Hyperion Press Limited, 300 Wales Avenue,
Winnipeg, MB Canada R2M 2S9.
Printed in Hong Kong.

For more information address Hyperion Books for Children,
114 Fifth Avenue, New York, New York 10011.

First Hyperion Paperback edition: February 1994

1   3   5   7   9   10   8   6   4   2

Library of Congress Cataloging-in-Publication Data
Czernecki, Stefan.
Nina's treasures/by Stefan Czernecki and Timothy Rhodes;
illustrated by Stefan Czernecki — 1st Hyperion ed.
p.   cm.
Summary: When Katerina runs out of food at the end of winter,
her beloved hen, Nina, saves them both by laying marvelous
multicolored eggs.
ISBN 1-56282-595-X (lib. bdg.) 1-56282-487-2 (pbk.)
[1. Chickens—Fiction.   2. Eggs—Fiction.] 1. Czernecki, Stefan. II. Title.
PZ7.C999Ni 1994   93-26932
[E]—dc20   CIP
                                                          AC

This book was set in 16-point Optima.
The illustrations were prepared in gouache.

Long ago, a little grandmother named Katerina
lived in a cottage near the village of Zelena.
The cottage was small and ordinary looking
but was surrounded by the most beautiful
flower garden that anyone had ever seen. In
the middle of the garden stood a henhouse.
Its sole occupant was Nina, who laid eggs
for Katerina.

All summer long Katerina tended her flowers. She cultivated and weeded with such care that her sunflowers were as tall as trees and her zinnias were bigger than cabbages. Hundreds of hollyhocks, peonies, dahlias, lupines, asters, and roses perfumed the air. Katerina loved them all, but her favorites were the poppies, for she used their seeds to decorate her festive breads and cakes.

Nina enjoyed the garden, too. It was the best place to catch moths and spiders and to enjoy an occasional ant or grasshopper. Nina pecked away all day. The more she ate, the more she wanted to eat. She even pecked at Katerina's sweet summer strawberries.

Every Saturday, early in the morning, Katerina went to the market. She gathered large bouquets of flowers from her garden and collected Nina's eggs in a basket to sell to the villagers.

Katerina always returned just before sunset. Her basket was filled with good things to eat—fine white flour and succulent sausages, thick sweet cream and smooth honey. She brought cornmeal, too. It was stored in the cupboard for Nina to eat during the long winter months when all the tasty bugs had disappeared from the garden.

One morning Katerina and Nina awoke to find frost on the ground. During the next several weeks Katerina picked all the fruits and vegetables and stored them for winter. She gathered the seeds from the flowers and put them in the cupboard, where they would be safe until spring planting. The poppy seeds were kept near the flour and sugar, to be used for Katerina's delicious pastries.

Nina had her own use for the seeds. Every morning she rose before Katerina and hurried to the garden to eat her fill. Katerina didn't have the heart to tell the fat little hen that they needed them all for spring.

The days grew shorter and the wind blew colder. Katerina and Nina watched as the last leaves were swept from the pear tree in the orchard.

Nina relined her nest with fresh straw, and Katerina hung her warm feather comforter out to air. The next morning it began to snow. Winter had come.

The outside work was done, and now Katerina spent most of her time in the kitchen. Her baking was popular with the villagers, and every Saturday morning she set off for the market with a basketful of her wonderful breads and cakes and cookies.

Nina was busy, too. She kept her henhouse tidy and laid eggs for Katerina's baking.

As the winter festival approached, Katerina was so busy that she forgot about baking something for her neighbors, who were very poor and had many children.

As soon as she remembered she rushed to the cupboard, only to discover that she had no more flour. What would she do? Her eyes fell on the big sack of cornmeal.

"Nina won't mind," she said. "I will make our neighbors some delicious corn bread."

Soon she was busy stirring up her favorite recipe. The oven glowed all evening, and at midnight she delivered a big basket of baked goods to the neighbors.

That winter was longer and colder than any that Katerina could remember. The snow was so deep that she could not get to the market. She could not even clear a path to the henhouse, and Nina had to stay in the cottage. Day after day Katerina and Nina sat near the warm oven and watched for signs of spring.

Finally Katerina had little food for herself and none for Nina. "If only I had not used so much cornmeal during the winter festival, at least Nina would have enough to eat," she muttered.

Nina clucked to herself. She did not want to worry Katerina. Day by day she grew skinnier and skinnier. Then she stopped laying eggs. Katerina tried feeding Nina the last potatoes and onions that she found in the cupboard, but Nina could not eat them.

"Oh, what will I do? What will I feed my little Nina?" cried Katerina. Then she remembered. She reached into the cupboard and pulled out a large sack. "Here, my darling Nina. Here is something you can eat!" she exclaimed, holding out her hand.

Nina's eyes opened wide. In Katerina's hand were the precious flower seeds for the spring planting.

Every morning Nina ate her fill of the delicious seeds, and every evening before bedtime she looked forward to a little taste of poppy seeds. Soon Nina was fat again, but she still did not lay eggs.

When the snow finally began to melt and the storks returned to nest on the chimney, Nina overheard Katerina talking to herself.

"What am I to do? I have no seeds to plant flowers and no flour to bake cakes and no money to buy either. I would never sell Nina, but even if I wanted to, who would buy an old hen that can't lay eggs? My darling Nina wouldn't even make a good soup."

Nina regretted having eaten so many seeds last autumn. Perhaps if she had thought of saving some then, there would now be a few left over. What could she do to help Katerina?

In the village it was time to celebrate the spring festival, and everyone was gathering in the square to dance and sing. Katerina could not go, for she had nothing to take— no food and no flowers. That night she cried herself to sleep.

The next morning Katerina was awakened by Nina's cackling and clucking.

What on earth is happening? she wondered. It must be a fox!

Rushing to the henhouse in her nightgown, Katerina saw Nina sitting on her nest, quite alone and quite safe. She was looking very pleased with herself.

"Have you finally started to lay eggs again, my little Nina?" asked Katerina as she gently lifted Nina off the nest.

Katerina was so surprised at what she saw that she almost dropped the poor hen. There in the nest were the most beautiful eggs. Each was different from the other, and each looked like a miniature flower garden laid out in gorgeous patterns of colors and borders.

Katerina put the eggs in a basket and covered them with a fine embroidered cloth. Then she set off for the village. This time Nina went with her.

When Katerina and Nina arrived, the villagers had already begun to show off the finery in their baskets. As each basket was uncovered the crowd cheered and applauded. Finally it was Katerina's turn, but when she removed the embroidered cover, there was complete silence. The eggs were so amazing that everyone was speechless!

Katerina traded Nina's beautiful eggs for everything they needed.

"I can get a sack of cornmeal especially for you, my darling Nina," Katerina said.

Nina ate the cornmeal and everything else that Katerina set in front of her. Nina liked being famous and pampered.

Katerina and Nina spent the rest of their days happy and comfortable. Nina never did lay any eggs like that again, nor did any other hen. Eventually the story of Katerina and Nina was forgotten, but not the marvelous eggs.

Today, before each spring festival, the grandmothers in Zelena work late into the night turning the most ordinary eggs into the most extraordinary treasures.